This book belongs to

_____

Published by Advance Publishers
© 1998 Disney Enterprises, Inc.
All rights reserved. Printed in the United States.
No part of this book may be reproduced or copied in any form
without the written permission of the copyright owner.

Written by Ronald Kidd
Illustrated by Peter Emslie and Niall Harding
Produced by Bumpy Slide Books

ISBN: 1-57973-009-4

10 9 8 7 6 5 4 3 2 1

Pinocchio

NOSE FOR TROUBLE

School was out, and Pinocchio was ready for
fun. He skipped down the street, swinging his books,
his heels skipping over the cobblestones.

Behind him, a small figure scurried along,
clutching an umbrella. It was Jiminy Cricket.
"Pinocchio!" he called. "Wait for me!"

Jiminy caught up with him in front of a small shop. That's where Pinocchio lived with his father, Geppetto. Geppetto carved all sorts of things out of wood — but his greatest creation was Pinocchio.

Jiminy hopped onto Pinocchio's shoulder, and the two of them went inside.

"Father, I'm home," Pinocchio called. The only answer was the tick-tock of a dozen clocks.

"Father?" said Pinocchio. He went into the
next room, and there, seated at a workbench, was
Geppetto. The clockmaker looked up, surprised.
"Hello, Son," he said. "I didn't hear you come
in. You know how it is when you're working."

Moving closer, Pinocchio asked, "What are you making?"

"A cuckoo clock," said Geppetto. "I even brought home a live cuckoo bird for a model. That way I can carve the cuckoo just right."

Pinocchio gazed at the bird. "May I take the cuckoo out of his cage and play with him?" he asked.

"I'm afraid not," said Geppetto. "You aren't the only one who's been watching him."

Geppetto nodded toward Figaro the cat, who was following the cuckoo's every move.

"Please?" begged Pinocchio. "I'll be careful."

Geppetto said gently, "I'm sorry, Son. We mustn't put the bird in harm's way."

Pinocchio spent the afternoon playing with his toys. Every few minutes he would glance up at the birdcage. He imagined what fun it would be to have the cuckoo perch on his finger.

At the end of the day, Geppetto went out to get some food for supper. As soon as he left, Pinocchio hurried over to the birdcage.

"Pinocchio?" Jiminy said. "What are you doing?"

"Taking the bird out for a visit," said Pinocchio. "Don't worry. Nothing bad will happen."

As Pinocchio reached for the cage door, Figaro
jumped onto the table.

"Watch out!" cried Jiminy. He looked on
helplessly as Figaro bounded toward the birdcage.
Figaro was fast, but the cuckoo was faster.

The bird hopped through the cage door and took off into the air.

Figaro, meanwhile, hit the side of the cage with a loud crash.

Pinocchio watched as the cuckoo circled the room. "See?" he said. "I told you it would be fine."

"I don't know," murmured Jiminy. "You shouldn't be disobeying your father."

The cuckoo darted in and out among the rafters, then began to investigate Geppetto's clocks. Wherever the bird went, it was careful to stay just beyond the reach of Figaro, who followed along on the floor below.

Jiminy climbed onto the windowsill to get a better view. As he did, the cuckoo turned and began flying straight toward him!

"Look out!" cried Pinocchio.

Jiminy leapt to one side.

The cuckoo hardly noticed, because he had
another target in mind. With a rustle of wings and
a happy cry, he flew past Jiminy and through the
open window.

As they watched the cuckoo soar into the sky, Geppetto walked in. He glanced at the birdcage and said, "Pinocchio! I told you not to open the cage! Now look what has happened! I'm very disappointed."

Panicked, Pinocchio looked around the room.
His gaze came to rest on Figaro.

"I didn't do it," he said. "It was Figaro! He
opened the birdcage and ate the cuckoo!"

"Figaro!" cried Geppetto.

He picked up the cat to scold him, which was lucky for Pinocchio, because at that moment the puppet's nose began to grow. It inched out farther and farther, until it was the length of a crayon.

Hiding his face, Pinocchio said, "Father, I think I'll go to bed early tonight. I'm not feeling well."

By the time Pinocchio hopped beneath the covers, his nose had grown another inch.

The next morning, Pinocchio was up before his father. He sneaked out of bed and ate a hasty breakfast. Then, throwing on his clothes, he headed for the door, calling, "Good-bye, Father! I'm off to school!"

Jiminy hurried along after him. He knew
Pinocchio wasn't going to school, because the
puppet's nose was still growing.

"Pinocchio," Jiminy said, "you must start telling the truth."

"I can't!" said Pinocchio. "I'll get into too much trouble."

Jiminy said, "You're already in trouble. Look at the size of your nose! Besides, don't you feel bad when you tell lies?"

"No, not really," said Pinocchio. As he spoke, his nose grew longer. But Pinocchio didn't notice, because he had something else on his mind.
He was determined to find the cuckoo.

Pinocchio hurried through the village, asking people if they'd seen the cuckoo. He climbed the bell tower, peering out across the sky. Next he bought a birdhouse and some seeds, hoping the cuckoo would stop by for a snack.

Wherever Pinocchio went, Jiminy Cricket
followed along behind, trying to talk to him. But
Pinocchio wouldn't listen to his conscience.

Instead, he told lie after lie — about why he
was out of school, where he was going, and what
he was doing. Each time, his nose grew a little
longer, until soon it was the length of a broomstick.

All the while he looked for birds. He found lots of them, too. Unfortunately, none were cuckoos.

At the end of the day Pinocchio's nose was longer than ever.

"Are you ready to go home?" Jiminy asked.

Pinocchio sighed. "I guess so. Maybe it's time I started telling the truth."

Pinocchio walked back through the streets of the village. Jiminy ran ahead to clear a path. At last they got home safely, with Pinocchio arriving several seconds after Jiminy and the nose.

When Pinocchio saw Geppetto, he said, "Father, I have something to tell you. Figaro didn't really eat the cuckoo. I opened the birdcage, and the cuckoo flew away. It was my fault. I'm sorry I disobeyed you. Most of all, I'm sorry I lied."

As Pinocchio spoke, his nose began to shrink. It became shorter and shorter, until it was just the right size.

"I'm glad you finally told the truth," said Geppetto. "And now I have something to show you."

He led Pinocchio inside, where something sat on the table, covered with a sheet. Had his father finished carving the clock? Geppetto drew aside the sheet, and under it was a birdcage — and inside the birdcage sat the cuckoo!

"Where did you find him?" Pinocchio asked.
"He found me!" said Geppetto. "I was working
on the clock today, and he flew in through the
window. I think he likes it here!"

"He should," Pinocchio said, giving Geppetto a
hug. "It's the best home anyone could ever want."

Just then the cuckoo called from inside its cage.
"I think our new friend would like some music!"
said Geppetto. He picked up his concertina and
began to play. Soon the kindly old clockmaker
was dancing around the room.

Grinning, Pinocchio lifted the birdcage and
joined his father. He was happy to be home, where
his father loved him and he never needed to lie.
And that's the truth.

Pinocchio would not admit
The wrong thing he had done.
And he kept on telling fibs —
He didn't stop with one.
To speak the truth is hard sometimes,
But in the end you'll see
That honesty, without a doubt,
Is the best policy!